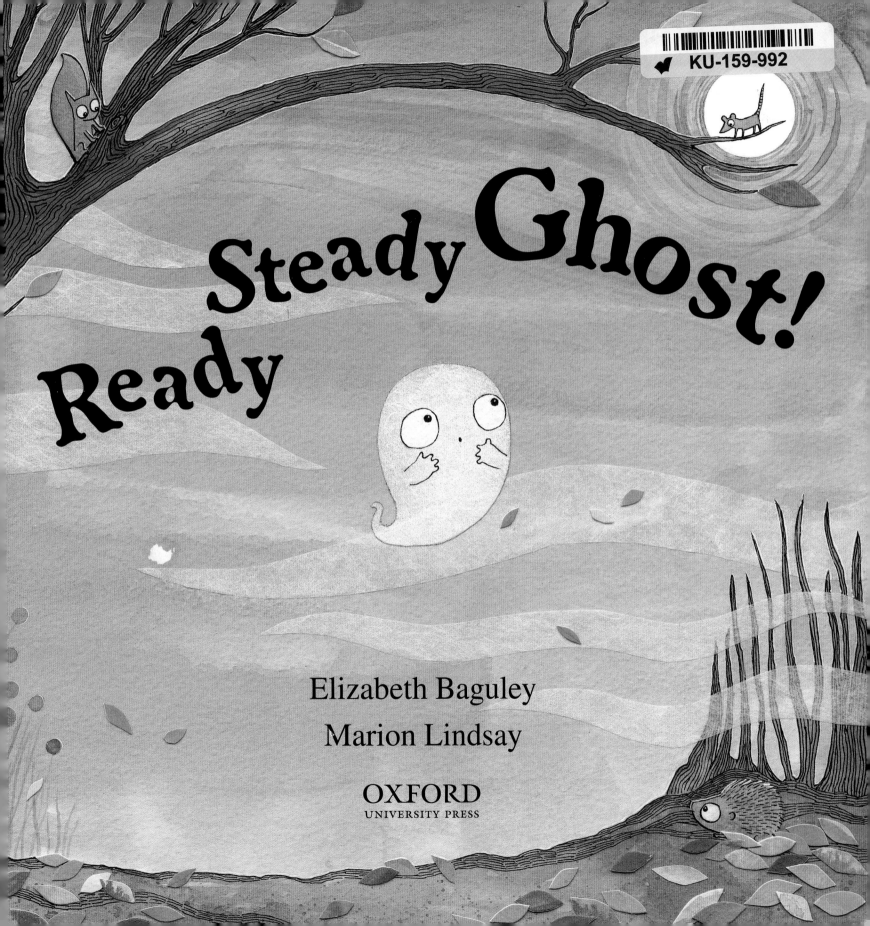

Ready Steady Ghost!

Elizabeth Baguley

Marion Lindsay

OXFORD
UNIVERSITY PRESS

Midnight!

It was time for Bertie to go haunting.

Ready, steady, *ghost!*

Bertie watched the big ghosts race off to
'Wooooo!' and *'Boo!'* in great forests
and tall castles. But Bertie wasn't a big ghost.
He felt far too small to haunt somewhere huge.

Bertie crept further into the wood. It was
darker than dark and lonelier than lonely.
'I don't like it out here,' he whimpered. *'I need to find
a homely house to haunt, a cosy house, a little house!'*

Two lights shone through the darkness.
'Windows,' said Bertie, hurrying towards them,
'on a little house.' Then the lights blinked.

'Shiver-me, shake-me!' said Bertie.

'Not windows at all but eyes that belong to a big, gobble-me . . .

Luckily, the gobble-me wolf
didn't see Bertie among the leaves.
It howled and was gone.

Something gleamed in the moonlight.
'*A path,*' said Bertie, hurrying towards it,
'*leading to a homely house!*'
Then the path slithered and slid.

'Shiver-me, shake-me,'
said Bertie. 'Not a path at all but scales that belong

to an **enormous, squeeze-me . . .**

Luckily, the squeeze-me snake
didn't see Bertie in the moonlight.
It hissed and was gone.

A twist of smoke curled into the sky.
'*Chimney smoke,*' said Bertie, hurrying
towards it, '*from a cosy house!*'
Then the twisty smoke was
lit up by a flame.

'Shiver me, shake me!'
said Bertie. 'Not chimney smoke at all but breath
that belongs to a huge sizzle-me . . .

Luckily, the sizzle-me dragon didn't see Bertie
between the trees. It roared and was gone.

Then Bertie saw more lights shining through the darkness.
'Windows — please?' he said. And this time he was right.
But they didn't belong to a house that was cosy or little or homely,
they belonged to a gigantic, freak-me . . .

castle!

Inside it was terribly tall and wide.
But Bertie hid behind a small door
to practise doing big-ghost things.

'*Boo!*' he said, jumping out as
ghostily as he could.

'Woof!' woofed a dog
who was lolloping past.

'*Shiver-me, shake-me!*' said Bertie.
'*I'm supposed to be scaring him away
not asking him to . . .*'

Bertie whiffled up the stairs. The dog
bounded after him, coming closer and closer.
Bertie shot through a tiny keyhole and into . . .

the attic.

'Shiver-me, shake-me, safe at last!' said Bertie.

'Eeeeek!' someone tiny squeaked.
'Who does that harum-scarum voice belong to?'

'*Just me,*' said Bertie. '*No need to be afraid, I'm only little.*'
'Then come on in,' said the little king and queen. 'Our castle
needs a ghost who fits and you look terribly scary.'

'*Do I?*' asked Bertie, feeling like a proper ghost at last.
'*Ready to haunt your house, your majesties,*' he added,
hurrying towards the little castle that was
homelier than homely and cosier than cosy.

So that very night little Bertie shouted big-ghost
'*Wooooos!*' and '*Boos!*' and,
to his delight, the tiny king and queen jumped every time.

Harum-scarum, shiver-and-shake-'em

— Bertie would never feel too small again!